THE TALE OF THE BLACK IGLOO

Another Adventure of Pepe and Pierre

A collaborative work by
Elizabeth A Lammers
and **Dan McKinney**

Illustrated by
Gabriela Epstein

PUBLISH AMERICA

PublishAmerica
Baltimore

First printing

ISBN: 978-1-60610-433-0
PUBLISHED BY PUBLISHAMERICA, LLLP
www.publishamerica.com
Baltimore

Printed in the United States of America

Dedication

E.A.L.
To my friends from the watering hole:
S.N.D., B.A.D, M.K.D., L.W.D.

D.M.
To my children, who listened
and my wife, who laughed

G.E.
To my crazy, but loving, parents

Pepe and Pierre are an unlikely pair,
One is a penguin; the other a bear.
Fast friends they've been through all their years
Through giggles, and tickles, and a few tears.

One summer day, when the days were long
They lay on an iceberg, floating along.
Then, Pepe jumped up, as you sometimes do,
When an idea appears out of the blue.
"With the white of the snow, and the white of the ice,
Wouldn't an igloo of black be nice?"

Pierre wasn't thrilled to leave his cool place,
As Pepe could see by the look on his face,
But out came the brushes, out came the paint
They painted all day 'til Pierre felt faint.

"It's time for a snack!" the tired bear cried.
So, Pepe put down his brush with a sigh.

"I'm hungry for salmon", Pierre dreamed,
"And some chocolate, vanilla, and tuna ice cream"
With three coats of paint on their little igloo,
As well as their hair, their clothes, and their shoes

Pepe proclaimed their work here was done;
They cleaned up their mess and went looking for fun.
They strolled to the neighborhood watering hole,
Where they joined their friends, a seal and a mole

They ate and they talked and they cooled off their toes
While the setting sun welcomed the moon as it rose.

After a day of such difficult work,
Pierre's eyes drooped and Pepe's head jerked

"I'm tired," said Pepe. Pierre quickly agreed,
"I'd like to get cozy in bed, yes indeed."

They walked 'round the lake and then they walked back.
Where was their igloo all painted black?

Could it have melted or drifted away?
It's not where they left it that hot, summer day.

Pierre tramped along by the light of the moon,
Wishing they'd find their little home soon.

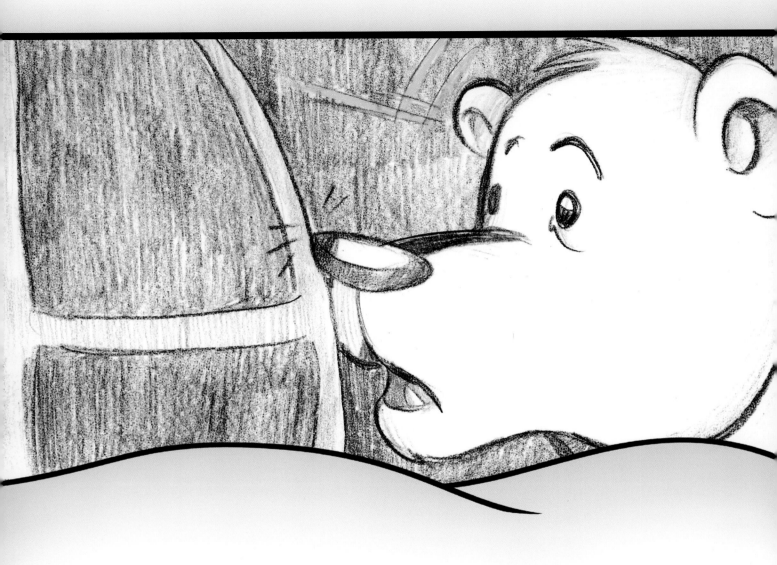

With a terrific bump and a loud "Oof!",
His nose was stuck to the icy roof.

Pepe stopped walking around and around
He looked at the sky and the lake and the ground.

As far as his eyes could possibly see,
The world was black, as black as can be.

"You've found it, Pierre!" he shouted with might,
"You've found our black igloo in the dark night!"

They jumped up and down with great delight,
Then put on their PJs and turned out the light.

Pierre rubbed his nose as he climbed into bed
"Tomorrow, Pepe, we're painting it red."

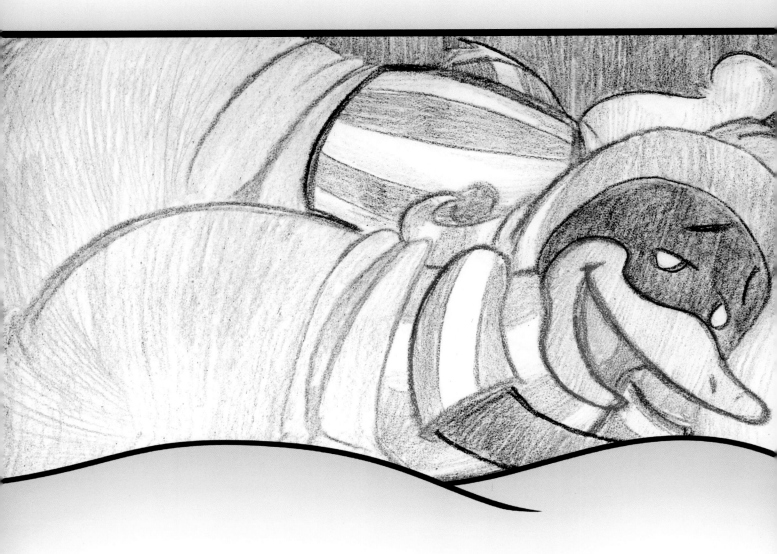

Pepe just smiled in his special way,
And whispered, "Today has been a great day!"

-The End-